ORCHARD BOOKS

First published in the USA by Scholastic Inc in 2017
First published in the UK in 2017 by The Watts Publishing Group

5 7 9 10 8 6 4

A CIP catalogue record for this book is available from the British Library.

ISBN 978 1 40835 185 7

Printed and bound in Great Britain

The paper and board used in this book are
made from wood from responsible sources.

Orchard Books
An imprint of Hachette Children's Group
Part of The Watts Publishing Group Limited
Carmelite House, 50 Victoria Embankment, London EC4Y 0DZ

An Hachette UK Company

www.hachette.co.uk
www.hachettechildrens.co.uk

POKÉMON PERIL

Adapted by Tracey West

ORCHARD

CHAPTER 1

MESSAGE IN A BOTTLE

"I wonder what kinds of Pokémon we'll see here in the Orange Islands," Ash Ketchum said. "I bet we find rare Pokémon that no one has ever seen before."

"We've already met some amazing new Pokémon," his friend Misty replied. "I can't believe we're riding on a Lapras!"

Ash smiled and patted the head of the large, blue Water-type Pokémon they were sitting on. He had befriended the Lapras, and the friendly creature had agreed to travel with Ash and his friends. Besides Ash and Misty, Lapras carried three other passengers: Pikachu, Ash's Electric-type Pokémon; Togepi, a baby Pokémon that

Misty brought with her everywhere; and Tracey, a Pokémon Watcher.

Ash had been to many new places and had had many adventures since he began catching and training Pokémon on his tenth birthday. But travelling around the Orange Islands was turning out to be the most interesting – and the most exciting – yet.

It started as a favour to his friend, Professor Oak. Ash had travelled to the islands to see Professor Ivy. She gave him a GS Ball, a mysterious Poké Ball Professor Oak wanted to study. Then his good friend Brock had decided to stay with Professor Ivy and help her with her work.

Ash was sad to leave Brock, but he soon met Tracey and found Lapras. He didn't know what would happen next.

"I certainly hope we find some new Pokémon on our journey," Tracey said. "It's always exciting to study something new."

As he spoke, Tracey sketched on a pad. The tall boy was a few years older than Ash. He always wore shorts and athletic shoes so he could easily keep up with any new Pokémon he found. And he always sketched what he saw. Ash peered over his shoulder. Tracey was sketching the Lapras. The drawing was a good likeness of the Pokémon, with its long neck, four strong flippers and hard shell on its back.

"You can study all you want," Ash said. "But I'm going to catch any Pokémon that I find." To become a Pokémon Master, Ash knew he would have to catch and train all kinds of Pokémon.

Misty rolled her eyes. "Ash, don't you

ever think of anything besides catching
Pokémon?" she complained.

"Sure," Ash replied. "Sometimes I think
about training Pokémon, too."

Misty groaned.

"Pika pika!" Pikachu
cried suddenly. The
yellow Pokémon
pointed at something
in the water.

"What is it,
Pikachu?" Ash asked.

Lapras swam closer
to the object.

"It's a bottle," Ash
said. "And it looks
like there's a message
inside!"

Lapras picked up the

bottle with its mouth. Its long neck craned around, and Ash took the bottle from it.

"Thanks, Lapras," Ash said. Excited, he quickly opened the bottle and took out a piece of paper. He unrolled it and read the message aloud.

"'If you know anything about a Pokémon called the Crystal Onix, please tell me,'" Ash read. "It's signed 'Marissa from Sunburst Island.'"

"A Crystal Onix?" Misty asked.

"It's an Onix made entirely of clear crystal," Tracey said. "Normally this Rock-type Pokémon is made of hard, grey rock."

Ash knew that. Brock had used his Onix often in battle. But a Crystal Onix?

"Is there really such a thing?" Ash asked.

"I'm not sure," Tracey said thoughtfully. "Several people claim to have seen it. It's probably just some tall tale."

"Well, I'd sure like to see a Crystal Onix," Ash said. "How about you, Pikachu?"

Pikachu nodded.

"Laaaaaaaaa." Lapras let out a low cry.

Ash looked. A small island jutted out of the water up ahead.

"That's Sunburst Island," Tracey said.

"Whoever sent that message lives on Sunburst Island," Misty pointed out.

Ash didn't have to think twice. He was looking for an opportunity to find new Pokémon, and one had fallen right into his lap.

"Next stop, Sunburst Island!" Ash cried. "Let's go find that Crystal Onix."

CHAPTER 2

THE SEARCH BEGINS

"Officer Jenny said that Marissa could be found in a crystal shop on this street," Ash said. "But every shop on this street *is* a crystal shop!"

Ash looked up and down the street, perplexed. After Lapras landed on Sunburst Island, they had headed right into town.

Ash couldn't wait to find the person who wrote that note.

"Sunburst Island is famous for its crystal," Tracey explained. "Most of the island's inhabitants are glass artisans. Their work draws a lot of tourists."

Ash pressed his face against the window of a nearby shop. Crystal goblets and vases glittered in a glass case.

"This stuff is pretty nice," Ash admitted.

"Pika!" Pikachu agreed.

Then a gruff voice startled Ash. "Face it, Marissa. Your brother might as well close his store for good. He doesn't even have anything to sell."

Marissa. That's who we're looking for! Ash thought. He turned around.

The voice belonged to a surly shopkeeper wearing an apron. He was talking to a little girl in pigtails.

"Don't say anything about my big brother!" said the girl defiantly.

Ash stepped between them.

"Are you Marissa?" he asked the girl.

She nodded.

"I need to talk to you," Ash said.

"Come inside my brother's store," she said.

Ash, Tracey, Misty and Pikachu followed Marissa into a small shop. The window displays were bare. Inside, small crystal Pokémon figures were scattered on a work table.

Ash was curious about the figures, but he was more curious to talk to Marissa. He took the letter from his pocket.

"Did you write this letter?" he asked her.

Marissa's face lit up. "You found my letter! Can you tell me about the Crystal Onix?"

"Actually, we don't know anything about it," Ash said. "We were hoping you could tell us about it."

Marissa looked like she might cry. "I guess I'll never find out about the Crystal Onix," she said.

"Sorry," Misty said gently.

A young man stepped into the room. He was tall, with short brown hair.

"Is my little sister bothering you?" he asked.

"Not at all," Misty said.

"This is my brother Mateo," Marissa said.

Ash and the others introduced themselves. Then Ash took a closer look at the Pokémon figures. There was a crystal Pidgey, a crystal Poliwhirl, a crystal Geodude and lots of others.

"These are pretty nice," Ash told Mateo.

"Why don't you put them in your window and sell them?"

Mateo's face clouded. "Because they're no good. My grandfather used to run this store. He was very talented. But my work just can't compare."

Tracey picked up a crystal Dugtrio and examined it. "What's so bad about them?" he asked.

"They don't look like living Pokémon," Mateo said. "Grandpa's Pokémon looked like they might come alive at any moment." He paused. "It's because Grandpa had inspiration. He saw the Crystal Onix."

Ash perked up. "The Crystal Onix?" he asked.

Mateo nodded. "Its entire body was made out of crystal. Grandpa saw it when he was a young artist. After that he was able to make

one great work after another."

Mateo walked to a pedestal on the floor.
He pulled away a cloth covering the pedestal.

Ash gasped. A large crystal sculpture of an
Onix glittered there. It looked amazingly
real.

"If I could find the Crystal Onix, I might
be able to create things like this," Mateo
said sadly.

Misty turned to Marissa. "So that's why you put that message in the bottle," she said. "You wanted to help your brother."

Marissa nodded.

"We'll help you look!" Ash said. "If your grandfather saw it, it can't be too far, can it?"

Mateo nodded.

Tracey took a Poké Ball from his pack. "Venonat can help us track it."

He opened the ball. A fuzzy round Pokémon with big, red eyes appeared. It had no arms, and walked on two flat feet.

Ash and Misty had seen Venonat before, but Mateo and Marissa looked surprised.

"Venonat uses radar to

track objects," Tracey explained. He showed Venonat the Onix statue. "Venonat, find something that looks like this!"

Venonat's red eyes began to glow. They whirled around. Then they snapped into focus. The Pokémon hopped toward the door.

"Let's go!" Ash said.

The group followed Venonat through town, and then out to the beach. Venonat hopped along faster and faster.

"I think Venonat's found something!" Tracey said excitedly.

Venonat hopped around a sand dune. The others followed.

The Pokémon had stopped in front of a large group of round rocks. The rocks were piled in a long, snakelike shape. They almost looked like an Onix.

Tracey sighed. "Venonat's radar can only do so much," he said. "Let's try another Pokémon!"

Tracey opened up another Poké Ball. A round, blue Pokémon that looked like a mouse appeared. It had large ears, and a round ball on the end of its tail.

"It's Marill!" Ash said. "Marill has great hearing, right?"

Tracey nodded. "It can distinguish the cries of Pokémon at great distances," he said.

Tracey took a small tape recorder out of his pack. He slipped in a tape and pushed *play*. A long, deep cry came from the recorder.

"That's Onix," Tracey told Marill. "Find it!"

Marill's ears began to twitch. Then it turned sharply and started running down the beach. It stopped at the water's edge and pointed.

A small, green island sat about one hundred yards offshore.

"It must be on that island," Ash said.

"But Grandpa said he found the Onix on this island," Mateo said.

Marill's ears twitched with excitement.

"Marill must hear something," Ash said. "We've got to find a way to get out there."

"It might not be so hard," Tracey said. "The tide's going out."

Ash watched as the water slowly began to retreat from the shore. Soon a sandy path was visible in the water, leading from Sunburst Island to the smaller island.

"Perfect!" Ash cried. "Let's go!"

Ash ran down the path and the others followed right behind.

Suddenly, Ash felt the soft sand slip beneath him.

His stomach lurched as he plummeted into a pit.

They had fallen into a trap!

CHAPTER 3

THE CRYSTAL ONIX

Tracey, Misty, Pikachu, Mateo and Marissa tumbled into the sandy pit along with Ash.

Then two familiar voices filled the air.

"To protect the world from devastation ..."

"To unite all peoples within our nation ..."

"Team Rocket!" Ash cried. He looked up. A teenaged boy and girl in white uniforms looked down on them, smiling evilly. A small Scratch Cat Pokémon stood between them.

Ash knew them all too well. It was Jessie, James and Meowth, a trio of Pokémon thieves. They were always trying to steal rare Pokémon.

"Don't you guys ever quit?" Misty asked.

"Not likely," James said. "We've been tailing you."

"We know that the Crystal Onix is somewhere on this island," Meowth said.

"We'll steal it and bring it to our boss," Jessie said.

The three thieves ran away. "Thanks for leading us to it!" James called out behind him.

Marissa looked distraught. "They'll get the Crystal Onix!" she said.

"Don't worry, Marissa," Ash said. "We'll find the Crystal Onix before they do. I promise."

Team Rocket's trap wasn't too deep, and Ash and the others were able to climb out in no time. Marill's ears twitched again, and the Pokémon ran quickly down the path towards the small island.

Ash and the others followed Marill. Soon they all stepped on to the island's shores. Marill took off through a cluster of tropical trees.

The trees opened up into a clearing and a large cave. The group walked up to the cave entrance.

Ash gasped.

Meowth was hanging upside down from a rope tied to a tree.

Jessie was trapped in a metal cage.

James was stretched over a pit dug in the ground, hanging on and trying not to fall in. And a round, pink Pokémon was disappearing into the trees.

"We set these traps to trip you up," Jessie said.

"But they caught us instead!" James finished.

"And then that pesky Jigglypuff showed up," Meowth said. "We thought we were goners."

So that was the pink Pokémon Ash had seen. Jigglypuff was following Team Rocket. It would never hurt anybody, but its song could put you to sleep – fast.

"Help us out," Meowth pleaded. "We'll help you find the Crystal Onix."

Ash laughed. "No way! Let's go, guys."

Marill's ears twitched again. It jumped up and down excitedly and pointed to the cave.

"Is the Onix inside the cave?" Tracey asked it.

Marill nodded.

The blue Pokémon led the way into the cave. Tracey took a torch from his pack. The light shone on the cave walls, revealing crystal stalactites and stalagmites of all shapes and sizes. They were growing out of the rock.

"The Crystal Onix must be here," Ash said.

Marill stopped in front of a dark, round pool of water on the cave floor.

The Pokémon dived into the pool. The round tip of its tail bobbed on top of the water.

"Marill's tail works as a float," Tracey explained.

Ash was impressed.

Suddenly, Marill's head popped out of the water. Its ears wiggled.

"What is it, Marill?" Tracey asked. Marill pointed to a spot in the water.

Ash leaned over the pool and looked. Two white circles gleamed underneath the surface.

They looked like eyes.

"Something's there," Tracey whispered.

The water began to ripple. Ash watched as a large, crystal head rose from the water. Then a long neck. Then a body and a long tail.

"It's the Crystal Onix!" Ash said breathlessly.

The huge Pokémon towered above them. Ash had never seen anything like it. This Onix was made entirely out of huge, round crystals. Its body glimmered in the light of the torch.

"It's real," Marissa whispered. "I knew it, Mateo. I knew it."

The Crystal Onix stared at them. Then it

let out a loud roar.

Tracey took out his notebook and pencil. "I've got to record some observations," he said.

Ash took out a Poké Ball. "And I've got to catch it! Professor Oak would flip out."

But Mateo stepped in front of him. "I've dreamed of this day since I was a young boy," he said. "The Crystal Onix is mine."

Ash nodded and stepped back. In all the excitement, he had almost forgotten why they were here. He wouldn't interfere with Mateo's dream.

Mateo threw a Poké Ball. "Go, Cloyster!" he yelled.

A light flashed, and a Water-type Pokémon in a spiky grey shell splashed into the water.

"Onix is weak against Water attacks," Mateo said. "Cloyster, Water Gun!"

A jet of water exploded through the opening in Cloyster's shell. The water hit the Crystal Onix, but it bounced right off.

Mateo frowned. "Water Gun! Fire rapidly!" he yelled.

Cloyster shot six fast blasts of water at the Crystal Onix, one after another. Another

Pokémon would have crumpled from the assault. But not the Crystal Onix. The Pokémon shook off the water as if it were a few raindrops.

Tracey shook his head in amazement. "Crystal Onix are resistant to Water-type attacks!" he wrote furiously in his notebook.

The Crystal Onix glared at Cloyster. It reared its giant head and let out another roar. Then it swooped down, and knocked into the Water-type Pokémon.

The attack knocked Cloyster out of the water. It skidded across the floor of the cave.

"Cloyster, no!" Mateo cried. His little sister ran to the Pokémon's side.

Then the air was filled with the sound of two whizzing Poké Balls. Ash spun around. The balls exploded in white light, and two Pokémon burst out.

One was Arbok, a large purple Pokémon that looked like a snake. The other was Victreebel, a combination Grass- and Poison-type Pokémon that looked like a big yellow plant.

Behind them, three figures stepped out from the shadows.

"Team Rocket!" Ash cried.

CHAPTER 4

INSPIRATION

"We'll take our Crystal Onix now," Jessie said, sneering. "Go get it, Arbok!"

Arbok sailed through the air.

"Victreebel, attack!" James yelled.

The plant-like Pokémon swallowed James with its big yellow head.

"Not me!" James cried. "Get Ash and those twerps."

Arbok and Victreebel lunged at Ash and his friends. Misty threw a Poké Ball. "Go, Staryu!" she shouted. A Water-type Pokémon shaped like a large starfish appeared. Staryu zoomed through the air like a flying disc. It slammed into Victreebel and knocked it out.

"Pikachu, get them out of here," Ash said.

Sparks shot from Pikachu's red cheeks. Pikachu tensed, then let loose a huge electric blast.

The blast ripped through Jessie, James, Meowth, Arbok and Victreebel. They fell to the floor in a heap.

The Crystal Onix roared. It swung at Team Rocket with its hard crystal tail. The Pokémon thieves went flying out of the cave.

Mateo faced the Crystal Onix. "Now to

finish my battle," he said. He threw out a Poké Ball. "Go, Charmeleon!" The orange-red Fire-type Pokémon appeared in a blaze of light. Charmeleon looked like a lizard. A flame burned brightly on the end of its tail.

Charmeleon ran straight for the Crystal Onix. The large Pokémon blocked the attack with a storm of crystal rocks. Each heavy rock was aimed right for Charmeleon. The smaller Pokémon quickly dodged the onslaught.

"It's Onix's Rock Throw!" Tracey said in amazement.

"Charmeleon, Flamethrower!" Mateo countered.

Charmeleon's body began to glow a brilliant red. It opened its mouth, and an incredible wall of fire shot out. The fire spun around and around like a whirlwind.

The funnel of fire engulfed the Crystal Onix. The Pokémon's body glowed from the intense heat.

Tracey scribbled in his pad. "The Crystal Onix's crystal is getting red hot," he said.

The Crystal Onix began to sway. Its eyes started to close.

Then its massive body crashed into the pool.

"Mateo, you did it!" Marissa cried.

"It's fainted," Ash said. "Mateo, hurry up and catch it."

Mateo held out an empty Poké Ball. He started to throw it.

Then he stopped.

Mateo stared at the Crystal Onix. The creature's body was beginning to cool down. Its crystals shimmered once more.

"I don't need to catch it," Mateo said. "Just seeing this amazing Pokémon has given me all the inspiration I need."

Mateo reached out and stroked the Crystal Onix's head. "Thank you," he said softly.

The Crystal Onix rose up once again. It nodded at Mateo. Then it dived back into the water.

The friends headed back to town. Mateo invited them all to stay the night. The next morning, he had a surprise for Ash.

"I've been working all night," Mateo said. "The Crystal Onix has truly inspired me. Thank you for helping me find it."

Mateo held out his hand. In his palm was a tiny crystal figure. Ash took the figure from him. "It's Pikachu!" he exclaimed.

The crystal figure looked exactly like Pikachu, right down to its lightning-bolt tail. It seemed real, like it could shoot out sparks.

"Pika pi!" Pikachu smiled when it saw the gift.

Marissa hugged Ash. "Thank you for helping my brother. I'm glad you found my letter."

"Me too," Ash said. "But now we've got to go. We have all of the Orange Islands to explore."

Pikachu, Misty, and Tracey followed Ash back to the beach. Ash let Lapras out of its Poké Ball.

"All aboard!" Ash cried. He and the others climbed on to Lapras's back. Then the Water-type Pokémon swam out into the ocean.

It was a beautiful morning. Tracey worked on a sketch of the Crystal Onix. Misty played with Togepi and Pikachu. And Ash pulled his red cap over his eyes and stretched out.

"This is so relax— Whoaaaa!" Ash cried.

Lapras was rocking back and forth. Ash sat up. The once-calm water was rough and choppy. Strong waves circled around them.

"It's a whirlpool, a big one," Tracey said.

Ash leaned over. "Lapras, get us away from here!" he shouted.

Misty shook her head. "It's no use!" she yelled over the roaring water. "It's already got us!"

CHAPTER 5

RHYHORN RAGE

Ash clung to Lapras's back. The whirlpool pulled the Pokémon and its passengers closer and closer to the centre. A wall of cold water washed over them.

Then everything went black.

The next thing Ash knew, he was lying facedown on a sandy beach. He sat up groggily then looked around, alarmed. Where were Pikachu and his friends?

He didn't have to look far. They were all stranded on the same beach, even Lapras.

"Is everyone all right?" Ash asked.

Misty stood up, still clutching Togepi. "We're OK, I think."

Ash looked around. In the distance, sheer cliffs formed a wall around the island.

Tracey looked excited. "The cliffs, the whirlpool," he said. "We must be on Pinkan Island!"

"Where?" asked Ash.

"Pinkan Island," Tracey repeated. "It's this mysterious place surrounded by humongous whirlpools. Hardly anybody's ever explored it, so nobody knows what kind of Pokémon live here."

Tracey got a dreamy look in his eyes.

"I may be the first Pokémon Watcher to discover a whole new type of Pokémon," he said. "Come on, let's hurry!"

The Pokémon Watcher took off across the beach. Ash quickly got Lapras safely inside its Poké Ball. Then he and the others ran after Tracey.

As soon as Tracey reached the cliff, he started to scale it. Pikachu climbed on Ash's back, and Ash followed Tracey. Misty put Togepi in her backpack and did the same.

Luckily, the cliff had quite a few footholds, but even so, it was a tough climb. Tracey reached a ledge close to the top of the cliff. He stood on the ledge and looked over the top.

"I can't believe it!" Tracey exclaimed.

Ash scrambled to catch up. He stood on the ledge and looked out.

The cliff overlooked a flat plain. A large Pokémon was eating fruit from a tree. The Pokémon had a sharp spike on the end of its nose, and its body was covered with plates of what looked like armour. But the strangest thing about the Pokémon was its colour – bright pink!

"It's a Rhyhorn," Tracey said. "A pink Rhyhorn."

By now, Misty had joined them. "I don't think Rhyhorn are supposed to be pink, are they?"

Ash took out his Pokédex, Dexter. The small handheld computer held information about all kinds of Pokémon.

"Rhyhorn, the Spikes Pokémon," Dexter

said. "Rhyhorn is known for its physical power and its considerable offensive and defensive battle skills."

A picture on the screen showed a Rhyhorn, but this one was grey, not pink.

"Dexter doesn't say anything about the Rhyhorn being pink," Ash said.

"Wow!" Tracey exclaimed. "I've got to get a closer look."

Tracey scrambled over to the edge of the cliff.

"It could be dangerous!" Ash warned.

Tracey ignored him. He stuck his finger in the air. "Hmmm, downwind's that way," Tracey said thoughtfully, pointing to a clump of bushes. He got down on his knees and quietly crawled to the bushes, hiding himself there.

From the ledge, Ash watched as Tracey began to sketch the Rhyhorn.

Ash frowned. "I don't think he should be getting that close," Ash said.

"He's a Pokémon Watcher, Ash," Misty pointed out. "He knows a lot more than you do."

Misty's words stung. Ash didn't like to think that anybody knew more about Pokémon than he did.

Ash climbed on to the top of the cliff. "I know lots more than you think. Just watch me!"

Ash boldly ran across the field. "Hey there, Rhyhorn!" he called out. "How ya doing, buddy?"

The Rhyhorn stopped eating. It turned and faced Ash.

"See," Ash said. "I know what I'm doing."

The Rhyhorn pawed the ground. It snorted.

Then it charged right at Ash!

"Hey, I just want to be your friend," Ash told it, but the Rhyhorn didn't listen.

Ash turned and ran. The

closest cover was the clump of bushes that hid Tracey.

Ash dived behind the bushes.

"We should be safe here," Ash said, catching his breath.

Snort!

The Rhyhorn stood right over them. It lowered its sharp horn.

"Let's get out of here!" Tracey yelled.

Ash and Tracey took off as fast as they could. The pink Rhyhorn was right on their tail.

Up ahead, Ash saw Misty and Pikachu standing at the edge of the cliff. Misty held Togepi.

"Get out of the way!" Ash yelled.

But there was nowhere to run. Ash, Tracey, Misty, and Pikachu huddled together. They were trapped at the edge of the cliff. And

Rhyhorn was charging fast.

"I guess this is it," Ash said.

Right at that moment, Togepi wiggled its tiny arms.

The next thing Ash knew, he and the others disappeared.

And reappeared in front of a nearby fruit tree!

Confused, the Rhyhorn tried to stop. It skidded along the grass.

It was no use. Ash watched helplessly as the Rhyhorn plummeted over the cliff!

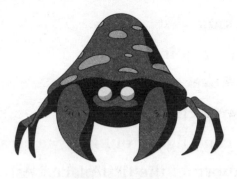

CHAPTER 6

THE SECRET OF PINKAN ISLAND

"Noooo!" Ash cried. He ran for the cliff's edge. Even though the Rhyhorn had charged at him, he didn't want to see it get hurt. Rhyhorn would have ignored them if Ash hadn't scared it.

Ash looked over the edge. The Rhyhorn was caught on a large tree branch sticking out of the side of the cliff. It was safe, but not for long.

The others joined Ash.

"Poor Rhyhorn," Misty said. "We've got to find a way to help it."

"I still can't figure out how we escaped the Rhyhorn in the first place," Ash said. "I think we teleported."

"But none of our Pokémon have the Teleport Ability," Tracey said.

Misty looked at Togepi. "I saw Togepi wave its arms right before we moved. Maybe Togepi has it!"

"Togi togi," the baby Pokémon gurgled.

"It couldn't be Togepi," Ash said. "Togepi's too small for such a big ability."

"I guess you're right," Misty said, but she didn't sound convinced.

The sound of a honking horn interrupted

them. A jeep skidded to a stop, and an officer jumped out. She was a young woman with blue hair.

"Officer Jenny, right?" Ash guessed. There was an officer named Jenny wherever they travelled. They all looked alike.

"Right," she replied, but she sounded angry. "This island is strictly off limits. Pinkan Island is a protected Pokémon reserve. How did you kids get here?"

"It was an accident," Tracey explained. "We got caught in a whirlpool and washed up here."

"And there's a pink Rhyhorn in trouble down here," Misty said. "We've got to save it."

Officer Jenny looked over the cliff. Then she snapped into action.

"We can pull it up," she said, taking several

strong ropes out of the jeep.

Officer Jenny explained the plan as she tied the ropes around Tracey and Ash. Then she tied each rope to the jeep. Tracey and Ash climbed down the cliff. They tied more ropes around the Rhyhorn.

"Just stay calm," Ash told the frightened Pokémon. "We're here to help."

The Rhyhorn didn't resist. Soon it was tied securely.

"We're ready!" Ash called up.

Jenny slowly reversed the jeep.

Ash, Tracey, and the Rhyhorn were slowly pulled up the cliff. Soon they were over the side, safe on flat ground.

Officer Jenny untied the Rhyhorn. "Are you OK?" she asked, patting its head.

The Rhyhorn nuzzled Officer Jenny. Then it hurried away.

"How come that Rhyhorn didn't attack you?" Ash asked.

"It knows me," Officer Jenny explained. "It's normally very shy around humans. Most of the Pokémon here are. They're not used to humans."

"Look at this!" Tracey

interrupted. Ash turned. Tracey pointed to Pikachu, who was happily eating a big pink berry. It was the same kind of fruit the Rhyhorn had been eating.

But Pikachu didn't look quite right.

Its tail was pink!

"Don't worry," Officer Jenny said. "It's just the Pinkan Berries."

"Pinkan Berries?" Ash asked.

"They grow all over the island," she explained. "That's what makes the Pokémon here turn pink. The Pinkan Berries only grow on this island, so it's the only place in the world where you'll find pink Pokémon."

Ash couldn't take his eyes off of Pikachu's pink tail. "Will Pikachu stay this way for ever?"

"No," Officer Jenny said. "Pokémon only stay this way if they eat the berries all the time."

"Whew!" Ash said. "I thought I was going to end up with a Pinkachu."

Misty groaned at the joke.

Officer Jenny packed up the ropes. "I believe your story, so I won't arrest you for tresspassing," she said. "But I do need to take you back to the ranger station to file a report."

"No problem," Ash said, relieved not to be in trouble.

They all piled into the vehicle. As they

drove across the plain, Ash kept his eyes out for more pink Pokémon. He wasn't disappointed. A herd of pink Nidoran, both male and female, grazed on a grassy field. A pink Rattata scampered between the trees. A pink Mankey swung from a tree branch. A flock of pink Pidgey pecked on the ground as a pink Parasect skittled by. It was amazing.

"I can't believe more people don't know about this place," Ash remarked.

"If the world knew about these rare Pokémon, poachers would swarm all over the island in no time," Officer Jenny said. "They'd put the pink Pokémon on exhibition, just so they could make money. That's why Pinkan Island is a refuge. We take good care of the pink Pokémon here. We can keep them safe."

Ash understood. "I can believe that people would try to steal them," he said. "They really are cool."

Just a few yards away, three Pokémon thieves were proving Ash right.

Jessie, James and Meowth hid behind some plants, greedily watching the herd of pink Nidoran.

"I've never seen anything like it," Jessie said.

"It's amazing," said James.

"This whole island is packed with pink Pokémon!" Meowth said. "We're lucky that whirlpool washed us up here."

Jigglypuff hopped past.

"Wow," James exclaimed. "A pink Jigglypuff!"

Meowth rolled its eyes. "Jigglypuff is always pink!" it said.

Jessie's green eyes gleamed as she studied the Pokémon. "If we capture all these Pokémon, we could open our very own theme park!" she said.

"We could call it Pinky Land!" Meowth said. "People would pay plenty to see the pink Pokémon of Pinky Land!"

James jumped up. "Let's get started!" he cried.

"Right!" Jessie threw a Poké Ball. "This is a job for Lickitung."

There was a flash of light, and a big pink Pokémon appeared. It had a long, sticky tongue.

"Amazing! A pink Lickitung," James exclaimed.

Jessie smacked the

back of his head. "James, Lickitung is always pink, too!"

"Of course," James said sheepishly.

"Enough talking," Meowth said. "Let's catch those pink Pokémon for ourselves!"

CHAPTER 7

NIDOKING'S RAMPAGE

"These pink Pokémon sure are incredible," Ash remarked. He and the others were looking through photos of the Pokémon that the rangers had taken. They sat on a porch outside the ranger station.

"That's why we have to be so careful to keep them a secret," Officer Jenny said.

"You are all free to go. But if I ever catch you here again, you're in big trouble."

Ash nodded. "We understand."

Suddenly, the wooden porch began to tremble beneath them. A loud rumbling sound filled the air.

Ash looked. A herd of Nidoran was stampeding across the ground, headed for the station. The normally tough-looking Pokémon seemed frightened.

Officer Jenny's face clouded. "Poachers," she said.

As if on cue, Team Rocket appeared over the horizon with Lickitung. They all looked frightened, too.

"We tried to capture these Nidoran for the boss," Jessie cried, running frantically, "but we got more than we bargained for!"

"What's going on?" Ash shouted above the

confusion. Nothing was making sense.

Officer Jenny raced out and herded up the Nidoran. They immediately calmed down in her presence.

Then Ash saw a cloud of dust swirling behind Team Rocket. The dust cleared, revealing a Pokémon. The creature stood almost as tall as Ash. It looked like some kind of dinosaur, with thick armour and a

long tail. Fierce-looking fangs gleamed in its wide mouth. A sharp horn protruded from its forehead.

Ash recognised it as a Nidoking, the evolved form of a male Nidorino. Normally, Nidoking was dark grey. But this one was pink.

And very, very angry.

The Nidoking stomped toward Team Rocket.

"Weezing! Smokescreen!" James cried, throwing out a Poké Ball. A black cloud with two heads poured out of the ball.

Jessie threw a Poké Ball. "Arbok! Wrap attack!" she yelled. Her Poison-type Pokémon burst on the scene in a flash.

The two Pokémon quickly sprang into action. Weezing belched out a thick cloud of smoke that engulfed the Nidoking. Arbok wrapped its body tightly around the Pokémon. Lickitung joined in, smacking the Nidoking with its long tongue.

"We've got you now, Nidoking!" Jessie shouted triumphantly.

"We've got to stop them," Officer Jenny said.

"We'll help you!" Ash said. He turned to Pikachu. "Give them your Thunder Shock!"

"Pika!" Pikachu nodded. It closed its eyes, and seconds later lightning bolts of electricity exploded from its tiny body.

The shock coursed through Jessie, James and Meowth. It knocked out Weezing and Arbok. It sizzled Lickitung.

The shock also hit Nidoking, reviving it.

The Pokémon roared and stomped its huge feet. It was angrier than ever.

Team Rocket tried to run. It was no use.

Nidoking grabbed them one by one and hurled them through the air. Ash watched as they disappeared over the horizon.

"Looks like Team Rocket is blasting off again!" he cried.

The Nidoking wasn't finished. It turned and looked at Ash and the others. It roared

loudly. Its eyes glowed an angry red.

"It still looks mad," Ash said.

"Team Rocket got it all riled up," Officer
Jenny said. "It's blinded by rage. We'd
better get out of here! Get in the car."

Officer Jenny hopped in behind the
steering wheel, and the others quickly
followed.

Jenny sped off across the field. The
Nidoking chased them with amazing speed.
It grew closer each second.

"It's going to catch us," Tracey said
nervously.

"I'll fix that!" Misty
said. "Go, Starmie." She
threw a Poké Ball, but
instead of her powerful
star-shaped Pokémon,
Psyduck appeared. The

confused Pokémon held its head.

Misty cringed. "Not now, Psyduck!"

Tracey threw a Poké Ball. "Maybe Marill can help us!"

The blue Aqua Mouse appeared. It took one look at Nidoking and disappeared back into its ball.

Ash reached for a Poké Ball of his own. But he was too late. Nidoking opened its mouth and a stream of white light shot out.

"Its Hyper Beam!" Officer Jenny said. "If it hits us, we're doomed!"

Ash braced for the worst. But then something unbelievable happened.

A blue light surrounded the jeep.

Then they all disappeared.

They reappeared again at the other end of the field.

The Nidoking stopped in its tracks, confused.

"Now's my chance," Officer Jenny said. "Get out of the jeep."

The others obeyed. Officer Jenny grabbed a rope and used it like a lasso. She drove up to the Nidoking and threw the rope around it before it could react. Then she drove the jeep in circles around the Pokémon. Soon the Nidoking was safely wrapped in the ropes.

"Amazing," Tracey remarked. "She stopped

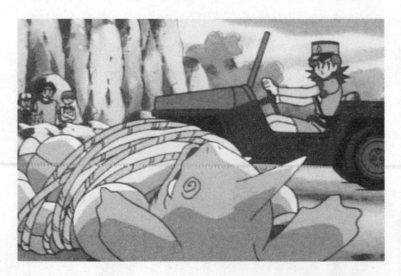

Nidoking without hurting it at all."

"I think it's amazing that we teleported before Nidoking could hit us with that Hyper Beam," Misty said. "I know this may sound weird, but I think Togepi did it. I really think Togepi knows some attacks."

"What makes you say that?" Tracey asked.

"When the Rhyhorn attacked us, Togepi waved its arms," Misty said. "And I think I saw Togepi wave its arms again when the Nidoking attacked. At least, I think I did."

Ash laughed. "Togepi's just a little baby. You can't do any powerful attacks, can you, Togepi?" He patted Togepi's pointy head.

Togepi just giggled. "Togi togi!" it said happily.

"Maybe whatever saved us is a secret," Ash said. "Just like the secret of the pink Pokémon."

"That's a secret I hope you'll keep," Officer Jenny said.

"We will," Ash promised.

CHAPTER 8

THE GRAPEFRUIT ISLANDS

"I sure could go for some fresh food," Ash complained. He and the others were once again sailing on Lapras's back. He'd been living off the dried food in his backpack for two days.

"Pikachu," Pikachu agreed.

Tracey peered through his binoculars.

"You may be in luck, Ash," he said, pointing. "Look!"

A cluster of small islands rose out of the distant water. Ash squinted. It looked like they were covered with tall, green trees.

"Those are the Grapefruit Islands," Tracey said. "All of the islands are supposed to be covered with grapefruit groves."

Ash licked his lips. "A juicy grapefruit would taste great right now. Lapras, let's go!"

Lapras picked up speed. In less than an hour, they were on the shore of the first island. They dismounted on to a small beach. A few yards ahead, Ash saw that Tracey was right. The beach was lined with tall grapefruit trees. Thousands of the round, yellow fruit drooped from the branches.

"They look ripe," Tracey said.

"And delicious!" added Ash. He reached up and picked one off a branch.

"Stop, thief!" a voice cried.

Ash spun around. A tall woman in a blue work uniform approached them. Her black hair hung down her back in a ponytail. She looked angry.

"A thief?" Ash asked. "We'll catch him for you!"

The woman grabbed the grapefruit out of Ash's hand. "You're the thief! The grapefruit thief."

"Wait a minute," Ash protested. "We're not thieves. Honest. We were travelling in the ocean and found your island. I was just hungry."

The woman studied Ash and the others. Then she nodded. "I'm sorry. I guess you don't look like grapefruit thieves," she said. She held out her hand. "I'm Ruby!"

Ash and his friends introduced themselves.

"Why are you so worried about people stealing the grapefruit?" Ash asked.

"We work hard to grow these grapefruit," Ruby explained. "It takes months of hard work. And then thieves come in and help themselves. It makes me angry."

Ash nodded. "I see what you mean."

Two men in work clothes like Ruby's ran up.

"Ruby, we've got a problem," one of the men said.

"A thief?" Ruby asked.

"Worse than that," said the other worker. "Follow us!"

They ran through the grapefruit orchard. They hadn't gone far when Ruby stopped in her tracks.

"Oh, no," she said softly.

A whole grove of trees was destroyed. Branches were snapped in half and strewn on the ground. None of the trees had grapefruit, or even any leaves.

"Who did this?" Ash asked.

"Only one thing could do this much damage," Ruby said. "A Snorlax!"

CHAPTER 9

STOP
THE SNORLAX

"It's over here!" one of the workers shouted.

Ash and the others followed the worker.
Then Ash stopped, amazed.

A massive Pokémon stood in the
grapefruit orchard. It was almost as tall as
one of the trees. It had a round, fat body.
It was mostly black, but its belly, face and

feet were tan. The Pokémon was breaking off tree branches and shovelling the juicy grapefruit into its large mouth.

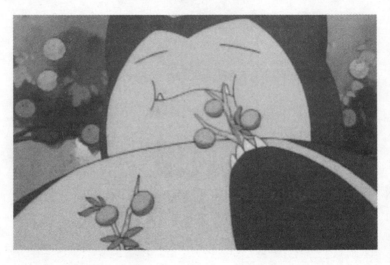

Ash took out his Pokédex. "Snorlax, the Sleeping Pokémon," Dexter said. "Snorlax isn't satisfied unless it eats at least nine hundred pounds of food per day. Once it is full, it promptly goes to sleep."

"Stop that Snorlax immediately!" Ruby ordered the workers.

The men ran up to the Pokémon and tried to grab the grapefruit branches out of its hands. But Snorlax punched them with its meaty paws. The men went flying backward.

"They can't do anything against it!" Misty said.

Ruby frowned. "If we can't stop it, we need to pick all the grapefruit before Snorlax gets to them." She took a walkie-talkie off her belt and spoke into it. "We need more hands out here. We've got an emergency!"

"We can help, too," Ash said. "I'll use my Pokémon."

Ash threw a Poké Ball. "Bulbasaur, go!" he cried.

A Grass-type Pokémon appeared. Bulbasaur looked like a blue-green dinosaur with a plant bulb on its back.

Ash walked to a group of trees that Snorlax hadn't touched yet.

"Bulbasaur, Vine Whip!" Ash commanded. The bulb on Bulbasaur's back opened up, and two thick, green vines shot out. They reached up into the trees and cleanly picked off two grapefruit.

Misty threw a Poké Ball. A Water-type Pokémon that looked like a starfish appeared.

"Staryu, you can help, too," Misty said.

Staryu flew through the air like a flying disc. It sliccd through the trees, chopping off the grapefruit in its path.

Bulbasaur and Staryu worked and worked. Before long, there was a big pile of grapefruit on the ground.

"Let's get these to Ruby!" Ash shouted.

But before they could make a move, a stomping sound filled the air.

Snorlax crashed through the trees. It plopped down next to the pile of grapefruit. Then it started shovelling them into its mouth.

"No, Snorlax!" Ash cried. "We picked those for Ruby." He turned to his friends.

"What should we do now?"

"We could beat Snorlax in a Pokémon battle and catch it," Tracey suggested.

Ash's face lit up. "All right! Bulbasaur, use your Razor Leaf!"

Green leaves with sharp edges zoomed out of Bulbasaur's plant bulb. Normally, the leaves would sting an opponent, causing it to faint.

Snorlax didn't seem concerned. It used a grapefruit to block the leaves. The leaves sliced the grapefruit into neat slices. Snorlax popped the slices into its mouth.

Then Snorlax stood up. It slammed its body into Bulbasaur. Then it sat on the Grass-type Pokémon, nearly crushing it.

"Bulbasaur!" Ash cried.

Snorlax stood up. It stomped off.

"Snorlax used Body Slam," Tracey pointed

out. "It's really powerful, isn't it?"

Bulbasaur was dazed but OK. Ash called it back into its Poké Ball.

"Let's find that Snorlax!" Ash cried. "I'm not ready to give up."

They followed the path of broken trees. Soon they came to the shore.

Snorlax stood on the beach. Ruby and some of the workers were there. They looked distraught.

"Snorlax has eaten all of the grapefruit on the island!" Ruby moaned.

"Thank goodness this is an island," Misty said. "Snorlax can't cross to the other islands and eat the grapefruit there."

Snorlax grunted. Then it waded out into the water.

Ash watched, speechless. Snorlax was swimming!

Tracey took out his notebook. "Amazing! Snorlax can swim. That explains how it found this island in the first place."

"We have bigger problems to worry about now," Ruby said. "I'll tell the people on the other islands to speed up harvesting there."

"And we'll try to catch that Snorlax before it does any more damage," Ash said.

Ash released Lapras from its Poké Ball. Ash, Pikachu, Misty and Tracey climbed on Lapras's back and set sail for the next island.

When they got to the shore, Ash was surprised at what he saw.

Snorlax was eating a huge pile of grapefruit. Next to the Snorlax were two angry people and one angry Pokémon.

Team Rocket!

"Stop eating our grapefruit!" Jessie yelled at the Snorlax.

"We worked so hard to steal it," James moaned.

Ash jumped off Lapras's back. "Not you again," he said. "Listen, why don't you just go away? We've got important things to do here."

"Buzz off, twerp," Jessie said. "If this Snorlax is going to steal our grapefruit, then we're going to steal this Snorlax!"

"You'll have to catch it first!" Ash said. "Squirtle, I choose you!"

Ash threw a Poké Ball, releasing a Tiny Turtle Pokémon.

"Squirtle, Skull Bash!" Ash commanded. Squirtle lowered its head and charged toward Snorlax. It slammed into the Pokémon. The attack had no effect. Squirtle just bounced off Snorlax's huge belly.

"How about this Pokémon?" Misty asked. She threw a Poké Ball, and a Water-type Pokémon appeared.

"Whoops!" Misty said. "I didn't mean to pick Goldeen."

Snorlax picked up the elegant Water-type Pokémon. It started to put Goldeen in its mouth.

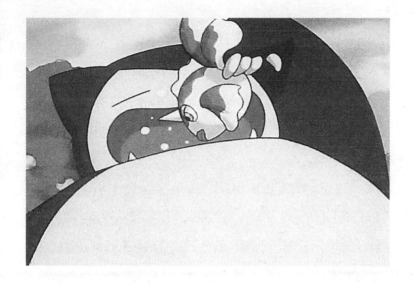

"Goldeen! Return!" Misty yelled quickly. She saved Goldeen just in time.

Meowth laughed. "You and your wimpy Pokémon can't do anything. We'll take over from here."

Jessie threw a Poké Ball. "Lickitung, go!"

The big pink Pokémon with the striped belly appeared. Its large, sticky tongue rolled out of its mouth. Lickitung tried to disable Snorlax with a Wrap.

Snorlax grabbed Lickitung by the tongue.
Then it used the tongue to wipe its mouth.

"You can't use Lickitung's mouth as a
napkin!" Jessie said angrily. She recalled her
Pokémon.

"Your turn, Pikachu!" Ash said.

Pikachu raced up to Snorlax. It exploded
with a Thunderbolt attack aimed right at
Snorlax.

But Snorlax was so big, the attack didn't

have any effect. The giant Pokémon kept right on eating grapefruit.

Ash was stunned. "Even Pikachu's Thunderbolt isn't working," he said. "I don't think there's any way to stop Snorlax!"

CHAPTER 10

IT'S SHOWTIME, JIGGLYPUFF

Tracey looked up from his notebook. "I think I know a way," he said. "Snorlax stops eating when it falls asleep. What if we put it to sleep?"

"Great idea!" Ash said. "But how?"

"Leave it to us!" James said. He took a watch on a chain from his pocket. He stepped in front of Snorlax and waved the watch back and forth.

"You are getting very sleepy," James said in a deep voice. "You're getting sleepier and sleepier. On the count of three, you'll fall asleep. One, two, three."

Snorlax kept on eating grapefruit. But James snored away.

Meowth shook James. "You put yourself to sleep, you nitwit!" it said.

"Let me handle this," Jessie said. "I'll sing it to sleep. *Rockabye Snorlax, eating grapefruit, when you are sleeping, you look so cute,*" Jessie sang.

James and Meowth joined in. Their singing was loud and off key.

Snorlax didn't like the song. It growled angrily.

Then it picked up a paw and batted Team Rocket like a tennis racket hitting a ball.

"Looks like we're blasting off again!" Team Rocket cried as they soared away through the air.

Snorlax stomped off in search of more grapefruit.

Ash shook his head. "Those guys never learn," he said.

"Maybe," Misty said. "But singing Snorlax to sleep isn't such a bad idea. I know one Pokémon whose song can put anyone to sleep!"

"Jigglypuff!" Tracey said.

Ash thought. "We know Jigglypuff has been following Team Rocket around since we came to the Orange Islands," he said.

"Maybe it's around here somewhere."

Misty frowned. "Jigglypuff always shows up when we don't want it to. And now we really need it!"

The sound of a motor boat interrupted

them. It was Ruby. She rode up to the shore and jumped out.

"Things are bad," she said. "Our radar shows that Snorlax is eating most of the grapefruit on this island. When it's done, it'll head for the third island. We'll have no grapefruit at all if we can't stop it!"

"That is bad," Ash agreed.

"To make matters worse, half of my workers are out of commission," Ruby said. "My foreman found them asleep. They all had pictures drawn on their faces with marker pens."

Misty and Ash exchanged glances. They knew that Jigglypuff got angry when people fell asleep during its song. In its anger, it drew on the faces of its sleeping audience with marker pens.

"Maybe Jigglypuff is here when we need it," Ash said.

"Then we need to lure it to Snorlax," Misty said. "I think I know how."

Misty got some supplies from Ruby. Then they walked to the opposite shore of the island. Snorlax would be there soon.

Ash helped Misty set up a small stage made out of wood planks near the beach. They hung Ruby's walkie-talkie on a pole so that it looked like a microphone. And they left some coloured markers next to the stage.

They needed bait for Snorlax, too. Tracey and Pikachu picked some grapefruit from a nearby tree. They piled it high.

When they were done, they gathered behind a low bush.

"Now we just have to watch," Ash said. "Watch and wait."

Snorlax was the first to arrive. It sat down next to the pile of grapefruit and began to eat.

"Come on, Jigglypuff," Misty whispered. "We need you."

Suddenly, Ash saw a tiny pink Pokémon hop on to the beach.

Jigglypuff!

Jigglypuff hopped along. Then it saw the stage and stopped.

Jigglypuff's large blue eyes lit up.

"Jiggly!" the Pokémon said happily. It hopped on to the stage. It picked up the makeshift microphone.

And it started to sing.

"Jigglypuff, jigglypuff." Its lullaby floated through the air.

Snorlax stopped eating. It yawned. The

lullaby was working.

The lullaby was working on Ash, too. But he had to fight it.

"Quick, Pikachu!" he said. "Thunder Shock!"

"Pika!" Pikachu was sleepy, but it was able to aim an electric blast at Snorlax.

This time, the blast worked. Snorlax slumped down, weakened.

Pikachu fell back, fast asleep.

Ash struggled to keep his eyes open. With every ounce of strength he had, he hurled a Poké Ball at Snorlax.

The ball opened and shot a beam of white light at the Pokémon.

Snorlax disappeared. The ball closed.

"I did it," Ash said. "I ... caught ... Snor ..."

Ash sank to the ground, fast asleep.

He woke up hours later. Ash rubbed his eyes.

Misty, Traccy, Ruby and Pikachu wcrc waking up, too. They all had coloured marker on their faces.

They looked pretty silly, Ash knew. But he

didn't care.

"I caught Snorlax!" he said, excited.

"Thank you," Ruby said. "Without you we couldn't have saved the grapefruit on the other islands."

Some workers came through the trees.

"Snorlax isn't on our radar any more," one man said.

Ruby explained what had happened.

"That's great," said the worker. "And there's more good news. The trees that Snorlax ate the grapefruit off are starting to bud already." He pointed to a tree.

Ash looked. Where Snorlax had broken off a branch, a leafy green bud had formed.

"I can't believe it!" Ruby said. "Our next harvest will be great. These islands will be covered with grapefruit once again."

"Snorlax may have the ability to help

plants grow," Tracey guessed.

Ruby smiled and shook her head. "That's the most amazing thing I've ever seen."

Ash thought about it.

So far on the Orange Islands he had seen an Onix that was made of clear crystal instead of hard rock.

He had witnessed Marill and Venonat's amazing tracking abilities.

He had seen an island filled with pink Pokémon.

He had felt himself teleport mysteriously. And now he had caught his very own Snorlax.

"I'm sure there are lots more amazing things to see in the Orange Islands," Ash said. "And I'm going to do my best to see them all!"

"Don't forget, Ash," Misty reminded

him. "You have to return that GS Ball to Professor Oak some time."

"And didn't you want to earn some badges in the Orange League?" Tracey asked.

Ash grinned. "No problem! We can do it all, can't we, Pikachu?"

Pikachu smiled and nodded with determination. "Pikachu!"

The End

DON'T MISS ASH AND FRIENDS'
NEXT EXCITING ADVENTURE

THE ORANGE LEAGUE

READ ON FOR A SNEAK PEEK ...

"Go, Lapras!" Ash Ketchum shouted to his Water-type Pokémon. The big blue creature sped across the sparkling ocean waters that surrounded the Orange Islands.

Ash and his friends rode atop Lapras's sturdy, round back. His longtime friend, Misty, held her baby Pokémon, Togepi. His new friend, Tracey, drew in a sketchbook. And Pikachu, Ash's Electric-type Pokémon, smiled and enjoyed the ride.

"I think Lapras is having fun!" said Misty.

Her orange hair blew in the ocean wind. She gave Togepi an affectionate squeeze. "And I should know! It is a Water-type Pokémon, after all."

Misty loved Water-type Pokémon. Even Ash had to admit, she knew more about them than anyone else he'd met.

"What's not to like?" Ash replied as he felt the warm tropical breeze on his face. "Being a Pokémon Trainer is a great life!"

Sometimes he couldn't believe how far he'd come since his tenth birthday. That's when he left his home in Pallet Town and began his journey as a Pokémon Trainer. He'd met a lot of people and had many adventures. But most important, he'd captured a lot of Pokémon since then.

"Pika-a-a-a!"

Pikachu's cry snapped Ash out of his

daydream. The little yellow Pokémon was flying through the air, thrown off balance by a surprise wave.

Ash dived after Pikachu, holding on to Lapras with his legs. He caught Pikachu just before it hit the water.

"That was a close one," he said.

"Pika," agreed Pikachu, its eyes still wide with surprise.

"We're not in a hurry, Lapras. You don't have to rush," said Misty.

"That's true," said Ash, "although I wouldn't mind getting something to eat."

"I'm kind of hungry, too," Misty agreed.

"Pikachu!" added Pikachu.

"Well, we're not that far from Mikan Island," said Tracey, a Pokémon Watcher. "I'm sure we can get some food there. And there's an Orange League Gym on the island."

"An Orange League Gym?!" Ash sat up, suddenly forgetting his hunger.

He had come to the Orange Islands on an errand for his hometown mentor, Professor Oak, the famous Pokémon expert. The Professor wanted Ash, Misty and their friend, Brock, to pick up a mysterious Poké Ball called the GS Ball from his old friend, Professor Ivy. Ash picked up the GS Ball, but he lost a friend. Brock decided to stay and help Professor Ivy.

Ash missed Brock but he soon found another friend, Tracey, and a new Pokémon, Lapras. And then he heard about the Orange League.

"I guess this is it, huh, Ash?" Misty said, knocking him with her elbow. "The beginning of a whole new challenge!"

Ash knew she was teasing him but he didn't care. He'd done pretty well in the Pokémon League back home. He couldn't wait to win the Orange League's four badges and then compete for the championship trophy in their league tournament. Misty could tease all she wanted!

"You just wait and see! I'm gonna be the greatest Pokémon Trainer the Orange Islands have ever seen!" Ash said.

"Pika pika!" Pikachu squeaked in agreement.

"See? Pikachu knows I'm right!" Ash said. "We're going to challenge every Gym Leader on these islands!"

Misty laughed and shook her head. "Too bad you don't have any confidence, Ash Ketchum."

Ash smiled at Pikachu. How could he not feel confident? He and Pikachu made a great team.

"Full speed ahead!" Tracey shouted. "Next stop, Mikan Island!"

READ
THE ORANGE LEAGUE
TO FIND OUT WHAT HAPPENS NEXT!

POKÉ RAP!

I want to be the very best there ever was
To beat all the rest, yeah, that's my cause
Catch 'em, Catch 'em, Gotta catch 'em all
Pokémon I'll search across the land
Look far and wide
Release from my hand
The power that's inside
Catch 'em, Catch 'em, Gotta catch 'em all, Pokémon!
Gotta catch 'em all, Gotta catch 'em all
Gotta catch 'em all, Gotta catch 'em all
At least one hundred and fifty or more to see
To be a Pokémon Master is my destiny
Catch 'em, Catch 'em, Gotta catch 'em all
Gotta catch 'em all, Pokémon! (repeat three times)

CAN YOU RAP ALL 150?
HERE'S THE NEXT 32 POKÉMON.
CATCH THE NEXT BOOK, THE ORANGE LEAGUE,
FOR MORE OF THE POKÉ RAP.

Alakazam, Goldeen, Venonat, Machoke
Kangaskhan, Hypno, Electabuzz, Flareon
Blastoise, Poliwhirl, Oddish, Drowzee
Raichu, Nidoqueen, Bellsprout, Starmie
Metapod, Marowak, Kakuna, Clefairy
Dodrio, Seadra, Vileplume, Krabby
Lickitung, Tauros, Weedle, Nidoran
Machop, Shellder, Porygon, Hitmonchan!

Words and Music by Tamara Loeffler and John Siegler
Copyright © 1999 Pikachu Music (BMI)
Worldwide rights for Pikachu Music administered by Cherry River Music Co. (BMI)
All Rights Reserved   Used by Permission

Gotta catch 'em all!™

WHICH POKÉMON DID YOU
FIND IN THIS ADVENTURE?

☐ VENONAT   ☐ RHYHORN   ☐ JIGGLYPUFF

Find information on these and all the other Pokémon
in the Official Pokémon Encyclopedia!

ENCYCLOPEDIA

OFFICIAL PRODUCT